Published in 1990 by G. P. Putnam's Sons,
a division of The Putnam & Grosset Book Group,
200 Madison Avenue, New York, NY 10016
Published simultaneously in Great Britain by Frances Lincoln Limited, London
Published simultaneously in Canada

Printed in Hong Kong
Book design by Debbie MacKinnon
Library of Congress Cataloging-in-Publication Data
Bradman, Tony.
This little baby.
Summary: A new version of the "This Little Piggy" verse
in which a baby enjoys the activities of a busy day.
[1. Babies—Fiction.   2. Stories in rhyme]
I. Williams, Jenny,   ill.   II. Title.
PZ8.3.B732Th   1990   [E]   89-70161
ISBN 0-399-22202-2

1   3   5   7   9   10   8   6   4   2
First impression

This Little Baby

Tony Bradman
Jenny Williams

G. P. Putnam's Sons New York

This little baby loves the morning,

this little baby waves bye-bye,

this little baby's getting dressed now,

this little baby . . .

starts to cry.

This little baby loves to cuddle,

this little baby wears a hat,

this little baby watches TV,

this little baby . . .

pats the cat.

This little baby's

VERY HUNGRY,

this little baby

has a name,

this little baby's feeling sleepy,

this little baby's

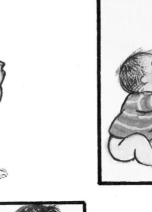

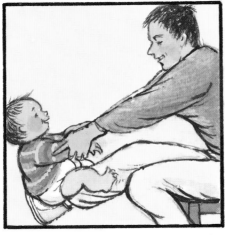

playing games.

This little baby goes to market,

this little baby comes home,

this little baby's got a favorite toy,

this little baby plays alone.

This little baby loves . . .

Mommy

this little baby loves . . .

Dad,

this little baby
loves bath time,

this little baby's being bad.

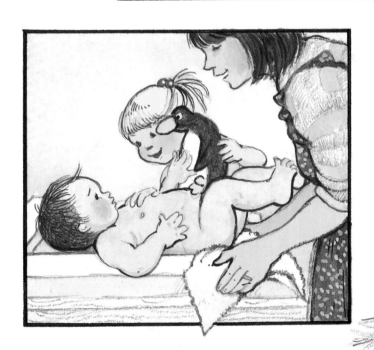

This little baby has a story,

this little baby has two,

this little baby's gone to bed now,

This little baby's just . . . like . . .

you!